THE WORLD
OF CHAOS

MurK
THE SWAMP
MAN

With special thanks to J.N. Richards

To David for going with me on my Quest

www.beastquest.co.uk

ORCHARD BOOKS
338 Euston Road, London NW1 3BH
Orchard Books Australia
Level 17/207 Kent St, Sydney, NSW 2000

A Paperback Original
First published in Great Britain in 2010

Beast Quest is a registered trademark of Beast Quest Limited
Series created by Working Partners Limited, London

Text © Beast Quest Limited 2010
Cover and inside illustrations by Steve Sims © Orchard Books 2010

A CIP catalogue record for this book is available from
the British Library.

ISBN 978 1 40830 726 7

9 10 8

Printed in Great Britain by CPI Bookmarque, Croydon

Orchard Books is a division of Hachette Children's Books,
an Hachette UK company

www.hachette.co.uk

MurK
THE SWAMP
MAN

BY ADAM BLADE

ORCHARD BOOKS

Hail, young warriors!

Tom has set out on a Quest of his own choosing, and I have the honour of helping with magic learnt from the greatest teacher of them all: my master, Aduro. Tom's challenges will be great: a new kingdom, a lost mother and six more Beasts under Velmal's spell. Tom isn't just fighting to save a kingdom. He's fighting to save those lives closest to him and to prove that love can conquer evil. Can it? Tom will only find out by staying strong and keeping the flame of hope alive. As long as no foul wind blows it out...

Yours truly,

The apprentice, Marc

PROLOGUE

Zenbar knelt down and tucked her thick leather trousers into her boots. Her gaze skimmed the rainbow swamp ahead, searching for the telltale flash of rippling scales. They belonged to the vipers that made these muddy waters their home, and they would be all too eager to sink their fangs into another unsuspecting victim. Only last week, Emni, Zenbar's friend, had been attacked while fishing here. He'd escaped with his life. *But not his leg*, Zenbar thought bitterly; that had been amputated because of the viper's poisonous bite.

Zenbar put her eel-catching box over her shoulder, grasped her staff and straightened up. In the pale light of the breaking dawn, she could see that Kayonia's swamp was completely still except for the muddy bubbles of red, blue and green which spluttered and popped.

She smiled, thinking of the other eel-catchers who were still snoozing in their beds. "I can sleep when I'm dead," she said to herself. "Right now, there are eels to be caught."

She strode into the swamp, colourful swirling mud covering her boots. Cold mist quickly surrounded Zenbar as she moved deeper into the bog, which made it difficult to see. She tried to use the small hillocks that poked through the swamp's surface but her feet kept sliding off. "I'll have to wade through the mud, as usual," she muttered. She used her wooden staff to test the depth of the swamp before taking each step.

Zenbar cried out as a searing pain suddenly shot through her calf. Her leg buckled beneath her but somehow she managed to stay upright. She looked down fearfully, expecting to see a viper circling her in the water – but there was nothing there. She groaned as more pain blazed through her other leg. She swiftly rolled up her trousers to reveal several leeches clinging to her legs. She winced as one of the leeches popped off her skin, its body engorged with blood, its mouth-sucker glistening red.

Zenbar's lips curled in distaste and she reached down to pull the other leeches from her legs. Blood tracked down her skin and she shuddered.

"If it's not the vipers, it's the leeches," she muttered to herself. "If it's not the leeches, it's the swamp, always looking for a way to suck someone und—"

Her voice caught in her throat as she felt something strong grasp her ankle and pull down. Her body jerked to one side and her right calf disappeared into the mud. Throwing her staff aside she grasped her leg, trying to heave it out of the swamp. "Come on, move!" she cried. Her mud-splattered cloak flapped around her body as she tried to free herself.

With a shock, Zenbar realised she wasn't sinking – instead the swamp was holding her prisoner! The rainbow bog tugged at her body with a force she couldn't resist, and she toppled onto her hands and knees.

With a scream of determination, she managed to stand upright. But now the lower parts of her legs were below the swamp's surface.

"Help!" Her wailing voice was swallowed up by the drifting marsh fog. "Please, someone help me. I'm trapped!"

Zenbar felt the mud tightening its grasp around her calves, the force sending tremors through her whole body. *What's going on?* Looking down, she tried to lift her feet free of the mud, but she froze as something strange and living emerged from the swamp. A cry of terror escaped her as the creature straightened up. Its body was a dripping mass of sludge, and decaying plants dangled from its powerfully built arms and broad shoulders. A chain of marsh weeds

hung around the Beast's thick
neck, and its head was large and
misshapen, covered with a thick
coating of slushy algae. Flames
flickered from its scalp like writhing
locks of hair.

Two eyes snapped open in the Beast's face, revealing an eerie red light. The force of the gaze pushed Zenbar to her knees. She sobbed, knowing that this swamp creature was worse than any viper.

The creature lunged forwards, foul smelling sludge spewing from its gaping mouth. With a squelching noise it oozed around her. Zenbar could feel the ice-cold mud enveloping her, suffocating her. With a sudden jerk, she was torn free from the bog. She screamed as her body was swung through the air, but the sound fell away as she was forced to look into the piercing red eyes of the swamp beast. The mud monster dangled Zenbar by her ankles and let out a screech of delight as he pulled her closer. She was about to be consumed.

I can sleep when I'm dead. Zenbar's words suddenly came back to her. Tears escaped her eyes and mixed with the mud on her face as everything went black...

CHAPTER ONE

GOLD RUSH

"Tom, back there in the gold mine, I wasn't sure we were going to defeat Fang," Elenna confessed, as she edged around a bend on the steep mountain pass. Silver, her wolf, raced ahead of her, clearly pleased to be leaving the dark tunnels of the mine behind. "Velmal's magic made him so powerful."

Tom gently pulled on Storm's reins

and led the stallion along a tricky part of the rocky trail. Memories of his battle with the mighty bat fiend filled his mind: the massive leathery wings, the gust of the Beast's foul breath, his sharp fangs. "The Beasts of Kayonia are the strongest we've ever faced," he admitted. "But we can't stop, not when my mother—"

Tom broke off, swallowing hard. Just thinking of how Freya was entrapped by Velmal almost suffocated him with rage. He knew she was nearing death with every passing day. If he didn't defeat the evil wizard, she wouldn't survive.

He gazed out across Kayonia, grateful that his eyesight had returned to normal. One of Fang's evil powers had been to steal people's sight. From their position on the mountainside,

Tom could see the whole land spread out below him.

It was not as beautiful as Gwildor or Avantia, but Tom was sure that Kayonia had once been a great kingdom. Queen Romaine could make it so again. He took a deep calming breath, remembering the magical ingredients from the six Beasts of Kayonia. These ingredients could make the potion that would save Freya and destroy Velmal's magic.

"Don't worry, we already have three of the ingredients," Elenna said softly. "The pearl, the jade ring and the red jewel."

Tom glanced at his friend in amazement. "How did you know what I was thinking?" he asked.

Elenna shrugged. "Remember how many Quests we've been on. Of

course I know what you're thinking!"
She gazed at him. "I came with you
to Kayonia so that we could save
your mother, and that's what we're
going to do."

Tom smiled at his brave friend,
recalling their adventures so far. With
Elenna, Storm and Silver by his side,
Tom felt like he could do anything.
Although he might be far from his
home in Avantia, at least he had
his friends with him on this journey.

He reached for the amulet that
hung from his neck and rested it in
his palm. He turned it over to see the
map of Kayonia – a map so real that
Tom could see the rivers flowing past
the mountains, and valleys etched
across the silver disc. He felt a rush
of excitement as he saw a fresh path
magically appear on the map. The

trail sped across the surface of the amulet towards an immense swamp in the north-west. The word 'Murk' appeared next to it in swirly writing.

"Where's the Beast's image?" Elenna asked.

Tom shrugged. During all of their Quests in Kayonia, the amulet had always shown them the form of Velmal's Beasts. "He must be hiding somewhere. We'll discover what Murk looks like when we reach the swamp. While there's blood in my veins, I will find and defeat this Beast."

They continued to make their way down the mountain, each taking turns to lead Storm. Silver ran out in front. Tom was relieved that the mountain trail was easier to descend than it had been to climb, and as the sun rose higher in the sky, he and

Elenna jumped into Storm's saddle and cantered onwards.

As they finally stepped onto Kayonia's flat plains and travelled along a deserted road, Tom felt Elenna's exhausted body sag against his. He gently nudged her in the ribs and she gave a yelp of surprise, sitting bolt upright in the saddle.

"Sorry about that." Tom turned in his seat with a grin. "But I can't have you falling asleep or you might slip off!"

Elenna yawned and stretched her arms. "My body has no idea what time it is. Nightfall in this kingdom is so sudden, I never know when to sleep."

"I can't get used to it either," Tom admitted, as they rounded a bend in the road. "I wonder how Kayonian people manage it."

"We'll be able to ask them ourselves." Elenna pointed ahead over his shoulder. "There's a village over there. We can stop for some food."

"And a rest," Tom added. "We'll both need it before we face Murk in the swamp."

Silver let out a howl of excitement and scampered into the village. Tom, Elenna and Storm followed. As they rode into the main square, people rushed to greet them, excitement lighting up their faces.

"Welcome, welcome!" a middle-aged woman wearing a headscarf called out.

"Why are they so happy to see us?" Elenna hissed.

"I don't know," Tom replied. "But we'd better find out." He jumped

out of the saddle and the villagers surrounded him, patting his pockets and peering into Storm's saddlebags. They did the same to Elenna as she dismounted.

"Where's the gold?" asked an old woman with several missing teeth. Her eyes were feverish.

Tom felt a jolt of alarm go through him as everything became clear. On their last Quest, he had destroyed the gold mine that Fang had lived in, and freed the slaves that worked there.

He'd thought that the imprisoned miners would be happy to have their freedom, but instead they'd been enraged that the kingdom's main source of gold had gone for ever.

Now he could see why. Tom looked around at the villagers. Men, women and children all reached out, grasping hands pulled at his clothes and fingernails scratched his skin. He turned to Elenna. "These people are desperate," he whispered. "They want gold, but we don't have any."

One of the villagers took a menacing step towards them and Tom braced himself for an attack from any angle.

"I don't think these people are going to take no for an answer," Elenna hissed as the villagers closed in. "What are we going to do?"

CHAPTER TWO

THE VILLAGE OF RUIN

Tom held up his hands in a gesture of peace. "Listen, please. We have no gold." He had to shout to be heard over the swell of voices, all calling out with angry questions. Storm whinnied in alarm and Silver gave a low growl as he looked at the furious villagers. Elenna knelt down and tried to soothe the bristling wolf.

'Well, what have you come to trade, if not gold?" demanded a woman with tightly tied back hair. Her gaze flicked between Tom and the angry wolf. "Fur, perhaps?"

Elenna gave a gasp of outrage and hugged Silver close to her.

"We're visitors, not traders," Tom said. "We have come—"

"Don't bother explaining." The woman's eyes were hard as pebbles. "If you don't have gold, I'm not interested."

An older man with a worn, brown face stepped forward. "My daughter does not mean to be rude. I can see that you and your friend are strangers to this land and so do not know our ways. We are waiting for the travelling gold traders." The man looked anxiously at the distant horizon. "Every week they stop at the gold mine, buy up the raw nuggets and then bring them here to trade before continuing around the rest of the kingdom."

The man rubbed at his temple with a wrinkled hand. "Because we're the traders' first stop, they always sell their gold to us for a good price. Look

around you, stranger. Their nuggets
are the only reason our village has
survived the crop failure of our lands."

Tom quickly scanned the
surrounding area. The village was
sat in the middle of parched
farmland. The earth was as dry as
ashes. He frowned, remembering the
farm he had grown up next to and
how the land had to be rested
between crops. It was clear that this
land had been over-farmed.

With Silver now calm, Elenna stood
up. "Tom," she murmured. "We need
to tell them what happened at the
mine."

Tom nodded and turned to the old
man. "The traders won't be coming."
Guilt flashed through him. "The
mine has collapsed. There is no
more gold."

"You don't look like a miner, so how would you know all this?" the woman with angry eyes demanded.

Tom swallowed hard. He couldn't bring himself to lie. "I know because I destroyed the mine." He swiftly went on to explain how he'd freed the slaves. "I'm really sorry," he finished. "But I couldn't leave those men enslaved."

"No gold," a young girl said, her voice cracking. "It can't be."

All around him, Tom heard cries of desperation as the news spread.

The old man sunk to his knees, his face crumpling. He picked up a handful of dust and held it out to Tom and Elenna. "Is this what we're expected to eat now? Without gold we cannot buy food."

"You owe us!" an enraged voice

called from the back of the crowd.
Silver let out a warning growl as the
villagers took a step closer.

"Tom, what should we do?" Elenna
asked. "Are we going to fight our
way out of here?"

"I don't know," Tom replied.
"These people aren't bad, but they
are desperate." He was going to say
more but he noticed a burly man
with an eye-patch watching them
coolly. The man stared, his bloodshot
eye never breaking contact. Somehow,
Tom sensed that this man was far
more dangerous than the crowd of
angry Kayonians. Tom's hand went
to his sword but a sobbing sound
stopped him. Looking down he saw
the old man was now lying on the
ground, crying.

Tom pulled him to his feet. He'd

wanted to help the slaves in the mine
but he never imagined that his
actions would bring such unhappiness
to others. Thinking quickly, he
reached into Storm's saddlebags and
held out a few pieces of dried meat.

The old man's daughter gave a
hollow laugh. "What good is that?
We need something to barter with.

Soon, the whole village will be starving."

"Wait, I have an idea," Elenna said. She reached into the bottom of her quiver and pulled out the coins that she had found in the jungle where they'd defeated Amictus the bug queen. She gave Tom a few coins and they hastily handed them out to the villagers.

Tom heaved a sigh of relief as he saw the Kayonians smile as they scrambled to grab the money. He gave Elenna a grateful look. "Good thinking," he told her.

She grinned at him. "Don't worry about it. We're a team on this Quest, remember?"

"I remember," Tom climbed back into Storm's saddle. "Let's go, we can't rest here."

Elenna climbed up behind him. "Good luck," she called out to the crowd. The old man was busy testing a coin between his teeth but he held up a hand in farewell, his eyes bright with happiness. Elenna and Tom galloped out of the village square and Silver raced by their side.

Once they reached the plains again, Tom paused and looked at the amulet. After memorizing the route, he guided them to a ravine that led straight towards the swamp.

Suddenly, he heard the distant sound of a rider spurring on his horse. Tom looked over his shoulder, spotting the blur of a horse and rider coming their way. Silver howled out a warning and Tom pulled sharply on the reins, halting Storm. He reached for his sword, but the rider was

already by their side; a muscular arm
snaked out and grabbed Elenna
around her neck, pulling her out the
saddle. Silver growled furiously and
Storm gave a high pitched whinny of
fear and bolted forward.

"Whoa, boy!" Tom said. He desperately pulled on the reins but his stallion plunged onwards.

He heard Elenna give a cry and looked over his shoulder to see her tumbling to the ground. She hit the earth with a thud and her scream was cut short. Her body lay twisted and motionless.

Was she dead?

CHAPTER THREE
SHOOTING STARS

"Elenna!" Tom shouted. Wheeling his horse around, Tom galloped back towards his friend's motionless body. The horseman had dismounted and was striding towards her, his mount now tied to a nearby tree. Tom couldn't help but notice how mistreated the horse looked. Its body was painfully thin and it was badly shod with worn horseshoes. As Tom drew closer to the horseman, he gave a gasp of recognition. *It's the man with the eye-patch,* he thought. *He must have followed us from the village.*

Tom snapped the reins and Storm cantered forwards, the wind making black ribbons of the horse's mane. Silver bounded over to his mistress and began to lick her face anxiously.

Tom felt the knot of fear in his stomach loosen a little as Elenna gave a small groan and opened her eyes; she had just been stunned by the fall.

The Kayonian was almost upon Elenna as Tom jumped out of the saddle and unsheathed his sword. "Leave her alone," he shouted. "Fight me instead."

The man laughed. "I have no interest in fighting you, boy. It's time to take what I came for. I knew the stupid fur-ball would run to his mistress's aid." He made a grab for Silver and the wolf howled and bared his teeth.

Elenna sat up and lashed out at the man with a clenched fist. "Tom, help!" she screamed. "He's trying to take Silver." The man grasped a handful of Elenna's hair and dragged her away from the wolf. She hit out again and they began to tussle in the dirt.

Just a few paces away, Tom tried to find a way to strike out at the man, but it was impossible to distinguish between his enemy and Elenna as they rolled around in the thick dust. "I can't risk hurting her," Tom growled in frustration.

Beside him, Silver let out a fierce snarl and leapt at Elenna's attacker, sinking his teeth into the man's forearm. The man howled with pain and let go of Elenna, and viciously punched Silver. The wolf fell to the ground. Elenna ran to Silver, shielding him with her body.

Tom stepped in front of the man, his sword raised. "I said, fight *me*."

The man removed an iron ball hanging on a chain from his belt. He twirled the ball above his head. "It's your fault that the gold mine was destroyed. You're a traitor to Kayonia." He sent the ball whirling through the air; Tom ducked as the chain snaked above his head. A moment later, and he would have been knocked out.

Keeping low, and dodging the heavy iron ball by weaving from side to side, Tom stepped forwards. The man dropped the ball and chain and pulled some metal discs with serrated points from his belt. Throwing stars! The sun glinted off their razor sharp edges as he sent them flying towards Tom.

Grabbing his shield, Tom thrust it out in front of him. He felt throwing stars embed themselves into the wood. He used his sword to bat away more metal discs as they spun past.

There was a high-pitched whinny
to his left and Tom turned to see that
one of the throwing stars had struck
Storm's shoulder. Dark bubbles of
blood sprung up on the horse's ebony
coat. The stallion snorted in pain, his
eyes rolling in their sockets.

"Tom, go to him," Elenna called over. "I'll cover you with my arrows."

"But—" Tom began, his glance returning to the man with the eye-patch. His enemy had run out of throwing stars and now clutched a short-sword. He gave a roar and ran towards Tom.

"It's all right, I can hold him back," Elenna yelled.

Tom sheathed his sword and dashed over to Storm, pulling the cruel star out of his flesh. Luckily, the wound wasn't deadly. Storm nuzzled Tom's shoulder gratefully.

Silver suddenly gave a low whine and Tom turned. The man had Elenna in his grasp, her arm twisted behind her back and her arrows scattered on the ground.

Tom could see the pain etched on

his friend's face as the man twisted her arm even more viciously. There was a cracking sound and Elenna screamed with agony.

"Let her go," Tom demanded, holding his sword ready.

Grinning, the man raised his sword to Elenna's throat. "Make me."

A cool anger took Tom over, giving him new icy focus and confidence. "While there's blood in my veins, I will stop you," he said. Tom threw his sword, sending it flying through the air straight towards Elenna's attacker. Startled, the man threw Elenna to the ground and dived out of the way. Elenna let out a sob of pain and cradled her arm, while Silver leapt at their enemy again, teeth bared. This time the man thrust his left knee into Silver's open jaw and the wolf yelped in surprise and agony, his legs buckling beneath him. As Silver released his grip, the fabric of the man's trousers tore and Tom saw that their attacker had a wooden leg.

The man laughed uproariously, swiftly gathered the dazed Silver up, and slung him over his shoulder. Untroubled by the weight of the wolf, the man climbed into his horse's saddle. "His pelt will be worth plenty," he shouted at Tom who had run to pick his sword up from the ground. "By Kayonia's three moons, it's almost worth all this effort!"

He laughed again and the horse galloped away down the gorge. Soon all that was left behind was a cloud of dust. Silver had been kidnapped!

CHAPTER FOUR

SNAKE ATTACK

Tom sheathed his sword, ran to Elenna and helped her to sit up.

"We have to get Silver back," his friend cried. She reached out to pick up some of her fallen arrows but let out a gasp of pain.

Tom held her shoulder. "I promise you that we'll find Silver, but first I have to make sure you're all right." He felt her upper arm. Past the muscle,

he could feel the two jagged ends of
a broken bone. They were scraping
against each other.

"Tom, please do something," Elenna
pleaded, tears streaming down her
face. "It hurts so much."

Tom quickly took the green jewel, won when he defeated Skor the winged stallion, from his belt. He held the jewel over the injury and watched as the stone gave off a faint green light. The bulge of the shard of bone smoothed down.

"Thank you," she said, testing her arm out. "That is much better. Come on, we need to find Silver." Elenna sprang to her feet and swiftly gathered up her bow and arrows.

Tom healed Storm's wound then leapt into the saddle, followed by Elenna. They hurtled off down the gorge. Up ahead they could see the tiny figure of their attacker on his horse, the wolf still over his shoulder. As they rode, Tom swiftly looked at his amulet and the path that glittered on its surface. "He's taking the same route that's on the map," he shouted over his shoulder.

"That means he's heading for the swamp," Elenna called back. "He's probably hoping that we'll lose his trail in there."

"We mustn't let him out of our sight." Tom snapped the reins. But as he spoke, the sun plunged down through the sky like a stone, disappearing behind the horizon. Darkness swirled around them and sudden cold prickled at Tom's skin: night had fallen. Storm neighed anxiously, his steps faltering.

"No!" Elenna cried. "How are we going to find Silver now?"

"It's going to be all right," Tom reassured her, even though anxiety made his own heart beat faster. "That man can't see in the dark, either. He's

going to have to stop." He drew
Storm to a halt. "At first light, we'll
go after him. But for now we should
make camp."

Elenna sighed and slipped to
the ground. She reached into the
saddlebag and brought out a flask of
water and a piece of dried meat. "It's
hardly a feast," she said, "but it's all
we've got. We'll need our strength."

Tom dismounted and took a swig
from the flask, wondering for a
moment if the man with the
eye-patch would be kind enough
to give Silver any water or food.
Somehow he didn't think so.

After feeding and watering Storm
and settling him for the evening, Tom
and Elenna spread out their blankets
and lay down to sleep. All through the
night, Tom heard his friend tossing

and turning. Storm seemed just as restless, and he pawed at the ground.

Tom gazed up at Kayonia's three moons. The faint, eerie howl of a wolf echoed through the quiet of the night and Elenna jumped to her feet, suddenly awake. "Was that Silver?" she asked. "Did that sound like him?"

Tom shook his head. "Silver isn't wild. He'd never howl into the night like that."

Elenna nodded wearily and dropped back to the ground.

"We'll find him tomorrow," Tom vowed. He closed his eyes and tried to sleep. *I hope I'm right*, he thought. He didn't want to break his promise to Elenna, not when Silver's life depended on it.

As the first hint of pink touched the sky, Elenna and Tom packed up camp, mounted Storm and were quickly on their way. Tom wondered what the new day would bring. He knew that they had to save Silver first, but would they face Murk today, as well?

"I still can't see Silver," Elenna said from her seat behind him in the saddle. The sun was high in the sky and beat down on them fiercely.

Tom frowned. He sat up a bit straighter and looked down the dusty path they were galloping along. He frowned as he spotted some recently made hoof prints. Each print had jagged chinks running across it.

"Look at the ground," he shouted over his shoulder. "A horse has been here recently – a poorly shod horse." Tom suddenly remembered the mistreated stallion that the man with the eye-patch had ridden. "Silver's kidnapper has been here recently." He paused and flipped the amulet around to the map. "The swamp isn't far either. That's got to be where he's heading."

Soon the path underfoot became muddy and slushy and the trees that lined the trail gave way to scrubby bushes. They had arrived at the edge of the swamp. But there was no sign of Silver or his kidnapper. Tom dismounted and looked more closely at the swamp. It was unlike anything he'd ever seen before. The mud at his feet was sometimes purple, sometimes green – changing colour in the sunshine like oil on water. Yet more bubbles of colour, reds and yellows, erupted and spluttered on the surface.

"I've never seen a rainbow swamp before," Elenna said from the saddle. "Do you think it's safe to cross?"

"I'll find out," Tom told her. He pulled his magic compass from Storm's saddlebag. It would tell him whether destiny or danger lay ahead. He held the compass out to the swamp and the needle strongly swerved to point to 'Destiny'. "We go straight ahead," he told Elenna. "We've travelled across a freezing desert in Kayonia, a rainbow swamp can't be much more dangerous."

"Silver is in terrible danger," Elenna said, her voice catching. "We have to find him."

Tom gazed out across the swamp. Elenna's faithful friend was out there somewhere. So was Murk. Tom knew he had to defeat the Beast if he was going to destroy Velmal's magic. The swamp ahead was completely deserted except for a single bare tree, seventy or so paces away. Tom narrowed his eyes. The tree was tall enough to give him and Elenna a good viewpoint of the whole area. They might be able to spot Silver – or maybe even Murk.

He turned to Elenna. "We should head for the tree," he said and quickly told her his plan. His friend nodded.

Tom settled Storm at the edge of the swamp. "Stay here, my friend," he said, patting the horse's flank. "I'll be back soon." He and Elenna picked their way across the rainbow-coloured muddy flats, leaping between the rocks that broke the surface. Tom noticed a pair of mud-eels squirming through the swamp, leaving a trail of reds and oranges. "I wonder what else lives in this place," he murmured.

He suddenly felt something tightening around his leg.

"Look out!" cried Elenna. Tom jerked his head around to see a snake's glistening coils wrapped around his calf. The serpent's body reared up from the depths of the swamp.

"No!" he shouted, as he felt the coils squeeze tighter. But it was too late. A diamond-shaped head whipped towards him, its fangs dripping venom.

CHAPTER FIVE

FINDING SILVER

Crack!

There was a blur of sudden movement and the snake's head snapped back. It released its grip on Tom with a low hiss of surprised pain. Elenna stood beside the serpent with a muddy wooden staff in one hand, her eyes fierce. She raised the staff again but the snake had already disappeared beneath the surface of the swamp.

"Thanks," Tom croaked.

"It's lucky I saw this staff in the mud," Elenna told him. She held out her other hand in which she grasped a square of thick canvas. "I found this as well but I'm not sure what it is." She handed it to Tom.

Tom unfolded the canvas and it sprung into a rigid cube. Peering inside it, Tom could see a fine bamboo frame sewn into the material. "It's a collapsing box," he explained. "I wonder what this and the staff are doing in the swamp."

Elenna shrugged. They continued across the swamp, their legs aching as they jumped from one algae covered mound to the next. Finally they arrived at the tree. Its windswept branches were bare of leaves and Tom could see that the twisted trunk had died a long time ago. "This tree's old, and the wood will be brittle. It will only take the weight of one of us," he said.

"You go," Elenna urged. "Just make sure you step lightly and spread your weight."

Tom nodded. He hauled himself up the decaying trunk and climbed amongst the fragile branches, stepping gently on each limb.

"What's out there?" Elenna asked as he reached the top of the tree. "Can you see Silver?"

Tom scanned the horizon to his right. All he could see were acres of flat, empty bog. He turned around in the tree, scouring the muddy rainbow-flats, and froze. There, about one hundred paces away, was the man who had attacked them. He was still on his horse and had Silver on a leash made of knotted vines. He was pulling on it cruelly, but at least the wolf was alive!

"I can see Silver," Tom cried out eagerly. "They're—" He broke off as he spotted the sludge near Silver beginning to froth and spurt. A mass of mud, laced with slimy reeds suddenly sprung upwards, towering over the startled man and Silver.

Tom heard the wolf give a howl of fear as the mass began to widen and a pair of muddy arms thrust out of the swamp water. "Murk," Tom murmured to himself. "It has to be." He felt his chest tighten with anxiety.

The man with the eye-patch let out a scream and quickly shoved Silver towards the giant pillar of mud, before galloping off on his horse across the swamp. Would the Beast attack Silver? Tom breathed a sigh of relief as the mass of mud dropped back into the swamp, leaving the surface still and flat once again. The wolf was safe, for now at least, but Tom knew he'd just had his first glimpse of Murk. *And I'm sure it won't be my last*, he thought grimly.

"What's going on?" Elenna called from below.

Tom scrambled out of the tree and dropped to the ground. He quickly told Elenna what he'd seen.

"We've got to get to Silver." Elenna started off at a run. "He's all alone and Murk might come back."

Tom looked back at the bank where Storm stood. "Stay there, boy, we're going to get Silver," he called. He and Elenna raced across the swamp, leaping from hillock to mossy rock.

"We're coming, Silver!" Elenna called out, as she spotted him in the distance standing on a small mound. The wolf let out a howl of happiness and put out a paw to run over to them. He yelped in terror as his whole leg disappeared into the mud.

"Stay!" Elenna bellowed, her face pinched with fear. Silver whined anxiously but remained where he was.

As they moved across the swamp, they tried to stick to the small hillocks, using them as stepping stones, but their feet kept sliding off.

"We're moving too slowly," Tom said with frustration. "We'll have to go through the mud."

"But what about the snakes?" Elenna asked.

Tom pointed to the staff that was still in her hand. "You dealt with that last snake, and we'll do the same to anything else that comes our way." His friend nodded and they plunged through the sludge. Tom saw something long and thin slither in the mud in front of him. Thinking it was another snake, his hand reached for his sword, but it was just another eel. The creature glided towards him and curled around his ankle. With a shudder, Tom kicked it off.

"Oh no!" Elenna exclaimed.

Tom turned to see his friend bending down and reaching for something in the depths of the swamp. "What is it?" he asked.

"I dropped the staff," Elenna said, thrusting her hand deeper into the sludge.

"I don't think you should have your hands in the swamp," Tom warned. "What if—"

Elenna gave a gasp and her face twisted with pain. She pulled her arms free of the mud. They were covered in blood.

CHAPTER SIX

PILLARS OF FIRE

Tom ran to his friend. As he got closer he could see several leeches clinging to Elenna's arms.

"Get them off me," she pleaded.

"All right, but you'll have to trust me." Tom reached for his sword.

Taking the blade between his thumb and forefinger he gently ran it along his friend's arm, cutting the leeches' suckers from Elenna's skin.

The creatures fell into the swamp with soft splashes.

"Thank goodness for that." Elenna's face was pale. "I thought they were going to eat me alive."

Tom pointed to the blood that trickled down her arms. "You're still bleeding." He took Epos's talon from his shield and used it to heal her wounds. All the while Silver barked anxiously.

"Come on, we need to get to him," Elenna said.

She and Tom tramped forward, but as they did so, a new night suddenly descended.

"Oh, come on, that's not fair," Elenna cried out. "It's not even the middle of the day, yet!"

"I don't think Kayonia cares about being fair. In this place, there are no rules," Tom said. He looked around cautiously. Instead of being surrounded by the rainbow colours of the swamp, he could now see quivering columns of orange light and spurts of blue flames coming up from the marshy ground.

"What are those lights?" Elenna whispered.

"Will-o'-the-wisps," Tom replied. "At least I think they are. They're natural gases that seep from the earth and spark into fire. My Uncle Henry told me about them once, but I've never seen them before."

"They're beautiful," Elenna said, her face illuminated by the wavering flames.

"And useful," Tom replied. "They'll light our way to Silver." The wolf let out a bark of excitement as they picked their way through the swamp. Tom could see him standing on the small hillock, Kayonia's three moons shining down on his grey fur.

In the moonlight, Tom spotted the stark white of bones sticking up from the mud. Elenna had noticed them as well. "What kind of bones are they?" she asked nervously. "Are they human?"

Tom crouched down and used his

sword to lever a curved bone out the mud. It was a delicate looking skull with a beak. He shook his head. "It's a bird, long dead by the looks of it."

"I wonder what killed it. Was it Murk?"

"Perhaps." Tom felt a twinge of fear as he thought about what the Beast was capable of. "Hang on, what are these things?" He pointed to several nuggets sparkling just under the surface of the swamp. The jets of fire that surrounded them seemed to light each one up. With his sword in his right hand, Tom plunged his left palm into the mud and picked up a nugget. It was a piece of silver as big as his fist!

"Real silver," breathed Elenna. "Perhaps the destroyed gold mine won't matter so much now.

The Kayonians will have something
to trade with after all."

Silver gave a yelp and Tom looked
up at the wolf, who was just a few
paces away. "Let's go," Tom said,
slipping the silver into his pocket. "I
think your friend is getting impatient."

Elenna nodded at him in the
firelight, her eyes suddenly anxious.
"He's probably nervous. We have no
idea where Murk went or when he'll
be back."

"Let him come," Tom said. "I have to fight him, if I'm ever going to save my mother."

"But at night?" Elenna questioned, taking another leap. She was just a few strides away from Silver now. "Murk will know this swamp better than anybody."

"We have fought other Beasts at night, and we'll fight in the dark again if we need to." Tom pushed on through the mud, weaving through the columns of flame. "But you're right, Murk knows this place better than anybody else." An image of the Beast suddenly invaded his mind: the immense, pulsing pillar of mud and reeds. "Murk is made from the swamp. That's why his picture never appeared on the Amulet."

But Elenna was not listening. She'd

climbed onto the small hillock where Silver stood and dropped to her knees. The wolf barked joyfully. Elenna wrapped her arms around him, burying her face in his fur.

The ivory moonlight that bathed Elenna and Silver suddenly disappeared. Turning around, Tom saw a column of mud towering out of the water. Murk!

Enormous shoulders made of slime appeared at the top of the pillar. Massive arms wrapped with reeds punched out of the reeking swamp water, while Tom watched powerful legs sprout. Tom's hand reached for his sword as a head burst from the top of the mud pillar. Two red orbs appeared in the Beast's face, as Murk's eyes snapped open. Flames flickered above the Beast's head.

Tom met his enemy's gaze but found that his limbs suddenly felt heavy and slow. *I've never battled anything like this*, he thought.

Murk opened his mouth and frothing mud oozed from between teeth ranged like leaning tombstones. From behind him, Tom could hear Silver howling, and the *twang* of a bow as Elenna loosed an arrow at the Beast. But Tom could not drag his gaze from Murk's red eyes. His hand refused to pull the sword from its sheath, even as the Beast loomed over him and lowered his massive head, his mouth wide open.

Murk let out a roar and stinking breath pushed Tom's hair back from his forehead. Tom tried to reach for his sword again but his hand refused to obey. *Why can't I move?*

he asked himself desperately as the Beast edged closer. *I'm running out of time.*

CHAPTER SEVEN

A RED-EYED GAZE

His eyes are hypnotising me, stopping me from moving. The thought whispered through Tom's head as the Beast's red gaze locked onto him. He forced himself to shut his eyes and instantly found that he could move. He raised his sword and lunged forwards, his blade swinging upwards.

The sword slipped through the mud like a shark's fin through water, and Murk laughed. His laughter was a squelchy, wet sound that made Tom shudder. He looked down at his sword. The blade was smeared with filth and water, but when he glanced up he could see no wound on the Beast.

He moved in for a second attack. Bracing his leg muscles for balance and power, he swiped his sword in a vicious arc towards the Beast's stomach. No! Again, his sword slipped through Murk, leaving no injury.

The Beast let out a growl and smacked down one of his spade-like hands. Tom hurled himself out of the way, rolling across the mud, only to see that he was heading straight towards one of the pillars of fire. With a cry, he swiftly twisted his body away from the scorching flames and crashed into the swamp with a splash.

"Tom, are you all right?" Elenna's voice called out.

He jumped to his feet. "I'm fine." Grasping his sword he turned to face the Beast again. Murk took a step towards him and Tom slashed out with his blade once more, attacking the swirling mass of mud, and slicing at the Beast's weed-wrapped arms and legs.

All of Tom's anger about his mother and Velmal poured out of him, powering the thrusts. He could hear arrows whistling through the air as Elenna aimed her bow at the Beast. Murk staggered backwards from the onslaught – but only for a moment. Tom's heart sank as he saw the Beast push forwards again. All of Elenna's arrows were passing straight through the Beast's body, and quickly sinking into the swamp. Murk bellowed loudly and lashed out with a fist.

"We can slow him down with our weapons but nothing hurts him," Tom yelled to his friend as he ducked Murk's mighty blow. "He's mud, not flesh and blood. We need to find a new way to figh—"

Tom suddenly felt his body jerk backwards, his feet dragging through the swamp. He twisted to face Murk. The Beast's arms were thrust forward and his fingers pointed directly at Tom. *I'm being drawn towards him,* Tom realised. *Murk isn't just invincible, he also has the power to pull people towards him against their will.* Tom was certain that if he got too close to the

Beast's body, Murk would enfold him forever, suffocating him.

Tom felt a grip on his arm. It was Elenna. The Beast clearly wasn't interested in using his powers to trap her as well.

"Hold on, Tom," she yelled. She gritted her teeth and pulled at him. Behind her, Silver, who still stood on the hillock, clamped his teeth on the hem of Elenna's tunic and together they heaved. Tom felt the force pulling him towards Murk weaken, until Tom and Elenna both fell backwards into the swamp.

Silver growled up at Murk. The angry noise seemed to enrage the Beast because the mud all around him swirled furiously, creating a swirl of sludge that flew up into the air. The curtain of swamp water wrapped around the Beast, adding to his bulk, making his arms and legs twice as big.

"I think he's getting ready to attack," Elenna yelled.

Tom nodded. By now, he knew

better than to meet Murk's blazing eyes directly, but he could see that the Beast's gaze was burning an even brighter red. Around Murk's neck, the chain of marsh weeds pulsed with a strange green light. They glowed with magic.

"We need to get those vines from around his neck," Tom pointed as he scrambled to his feet. "That's what Velmal has used to enchant the Beast. If we take it, Murk will be freed from the wizard's magic. He can just go back to being part of this swamp again."

"But how are we going to get it?" Elenna asked, staring at the Beast who continued to get bigger. "He's so strong, and getting stronger. We can't hurt him!"

Tom could see the Beast's limbs

swelling and extending, and he could hear creaking noises as Murk's chest and shoulders widened. The Beast grinned and Tom saw spaces spring up between the yellow stumps of his teeth as Murk's head grew wider!

Tom looked around desperately. There had to be a way to defeat the Beast and remove the chain of vines.

The people of Kayonia are relying on me, and my mother's life depends on it.

He was sure that the vines that enchanted Murk were one of the ingredients for the potion that would cure his mother, and break the evil wizard's magic.

Tom glanced over to the banks of the swamp, back from where they'd come. He thought of Storm and how lonely he must be in the dark. *At least he's on solid ground*, Tom thought grimly.

"Back on solid ground," Tom whispered to himself, an idea coming to him. "Elenna, that's it! If I can lure Murk out of the swamp, his body might dry out and become solid. Then I'll have an enemy I can actually fight!"

CHAPTER EIGHT

THE TRAP

By the light of the swamp's flames,
Tom could see that Murk was now
four times his original size! He let out
a roar.

"He's getting ready to attack!"
Elenna yelled.

"Time to put my plan into action,"
Tom said softly.

Silver barked and leapt at Murk,
continuing to distract him. The Beast

punched out with his mighty fists but Silver deftly leapt out of the way.

"How are we going to get him onto land?" Elenna asked. "We need something to lure him."

A whinnying sound cut through the mist and Tom looked over to see Storm picking his way towards them.

"Storm's coming to help us!" Elenna exclaimed.

"But it's not safe," Tom said. His horse gave a high-pitched neigh of fear, as the weight of his body made his legs sink into the mud. Storm was stuck!

"Stay still," Tom called. But his stallion was beginning to panic and thrashed about on the edge of the swamp, his head swinging from side to side. The stallion continued to sink and he gave another whinny of distress.

Murk turned and gave a mighty roar that sent more putrid mud rolling down his body. The Beast began to race towards Storm, cackling with evil delight. He was heading closer towards dry land, which helped Tom's plan. But...

"We can't let him get Storm," Tom yelled, chasing after the Beast. He jumped from hillock to hillock and by his side sped Elenna and Silver. Ahead, he could see Murk surging through the swamp, his giant strides soon leaving them far behind. The Beast would envelop Storm in mud at any moment.

"I've got to stop him," Tom said. He suddenly remembered the token that Tagus had given him. "I need speed," he told Elenna. "I'm going to use Tagus's horseshoe."

"Go," Elenna said.

He brought the shield up in front of his body and rubbed the token. He leapt forward, one foot pushing off a hillock and propelling him upwards. He somersaulted through the air, the night breeze stinging his cheeks. He bounded and leaped from jutting rock to small hummock, dodging the will-o'-the-wisps.

With his speed, he soon overtook Murk and reached Storm's side. He

gave his stallion a quick hug and the horse whinnied in greeting. "Now, I just have to get you out of here," Tom said.

The Beast roared in anger and Tom heard something hurtling through the air towards him. He turned to see the Beast shoot a streak of swampy gunk from his hand. Tom ducked the mud missile but slimy streaks peeled off and struck his face.

As Murk continued to stride towards them, shooting sludge from his fingertips, Tom knelt down beside his horse. He took his shield and placed it on the surface of the swamp in front of Storm. The stallion's front legs had sunk deep into the swamp, although his back legs were still on the solid ground of the bank.

"You must trust me, boy," Tom said,

as he held Storm's lower leg, and gently began pulling it from the mud. Storm stiffened, his flanks shiny with sweat, but Tom continued to talk to him softly. At last the stallion relaxed and Tom was able to pull his leg loose from the mud and place it on the shield. He quickly did the same with the other leg. Storm was free!

"Hurry!" Elenna's voice echoed across the swamp. Tom looked up and saw that Murk was almost upon them; Elenna and Silver were still a little distance behind him. Quickly, Tom guided Storm backwards onto firm land.

Tom grabbed his shield and turned to face Murk. The Beast had stopped and was watching him, seemingly unwilling to leave his swamp home. All around Murk, more mud bubbled, and the Beast increased in size.

"I have to get him to leave the swamp," Tom said to himself. "How can I make him follow me?"

The Beast held up his hands and two jets of mud rushed towards Tom; but he was ready. Holding up the shield, he deflected the mud and it surged back towards the Beast like a massive tidal wave, knocking him to the ground.

As the Beast wallowed in the mud, Tom saw Elenna and Silver leap onto the bank. "Take care of Storm for me," he said. "It's time I defeated this Beast."

Elenna nodded. "Good luck." She grabbed Storm's harness and carefully led the stallion away from the swamp's edge. Silver ran by her heels.

Murk was back on his feet. His eyes blazed with fury.

Tom raised his sword and the blade glittered in the light of Kayonia's three moons. With his other hand he mockingly beckoned the Beast with a crooked finger.

Murk's gaze flashed dangerously and his cavernous mouth opened wide to reveal scarlet gums and yellow teeth. A roar of fury came from his throat. The Beast barrelled forwards, his massive feet making the land shudder as he stepped onto solid ground.

Tom did not move. With a sword in one hand and his shield on his arm, he was ready to do battle. He heard a splintering sound and realised that the Beast's muddy body had slowly started to crack and dry out.

From the top of Murk's misshapen, algae-covered head to the bottom of his massive feet, the wet ooze of the swamp was turning silvery grey and shiny. Murk was transforming into a solid Beast.

The fight was on!

CHAPTER NINE

HIGH STAKES

Murk's mouth stretched into a grin. Tom leapt into the air and sent his sword slashing down. The blade raked across one of Murk's arms before sticking in a groove and wedging there. Tom heaved down on the blade and with a crack, the drying mud crumbled to the ground. He gasped as the Beast cried out in pain and then slowly raised his stump. Murk looked at where his arm used to be, the red light in his eyes flickering with uncertainty and fear. Then he looked at Tom with savage anger.

Tom met the Beast's glance and felt confidence surge through him. *I can look into Murk's eyes now,* he realised. His limbs no longer felt frozen when he stood under the Beast's gaze; Murk's ability to hypnotize had faded.

The Beast threw out his hand in an attempt to draw Tom to him. His muddy fingers trembled with the effort. Nothing! Murk quickly gave a roar of frustration. The Beast was weakened.

Murk lifted his remaining arm and curled his hand into a fist. He smashed downwards but Tom was too quick and leapt out of the way.

He twisted on the ground, thrusting up with his sword and hacked a chunk of mud from the Beast's leg.

From behind him, Tom could hear Elenna cheering. With a roar, Murk dropped onto his good knee. He pounded the ground with his remaining hand, again and again, making the earth tremble.

The tremors made it almost impossible to stand, so Tom had to crouch to keep his balance. Ahead, he could see the chain of vines dangling from the Beast's neck. "It's so close," he whispered to himself. "But if I can't stand, how am I ever going to get it?"

Murk roared with laughter as he continued to pound the ground. Each time he struck the earth he dragged his body a little closer to Tom.

"He's coming for me," Tom growled to himself. "I have to get to him first."

Thrusting his sword into the peaty ground, he used it to push himself upwards. Hurtling through the air, he thrust out his legs and kicked Murk in the stomach. The force of the impact sent the Beast toppling backwards, crumbs of dry mud

scattering from his body. Tom landed
on the Beast's chest, the mud
cracking beneath his feet. Murk was
crumbling away to nothing. But Tom
wasn't interested in completely
destroying the Beast; only in taking
the chain of vines. He knew that
once they were gone from Murk's
neck, Velmal's enchantment would
be broken.

He scrambled across the Beast's huge body and gripped the vines. With a mighty heave, Tom tore at them, just as Murk threw a giant fist straight towards him.

"Tom!" Elenna's scream echoed through the air.

Tom rolled his tired body out of the way of the incoming fist. As Murk's clenched hand slammed into his own throat, Tom saw dawn begin to break. Rays of light danced over Murk's prone body...

Coughing and choking with the self-inflicted injury, Murk half-rolled left. Then he leaned right. Tom felt a thrill of victory – the Beast was trying to roll out of the path of the sun, but it had him pinned. The area where the necklace of vines had been began to shimmer. The glow bloomed over the Beast's body, melting it into small silver-streaked balls of mud that rolled back into the swamp to disappear into the multi-coloured sludge.

Murk was defeated!

Tom looked down at the

enchanted vines in his hands. He felt a surge of hope. He had found the fourth ingredient for the potion. *Soon I'll be able to destroy Velmal and save my mother*, he thought jubilantly.

The air in front of him began to flicker and Marc the apprentice wizard appeared.

"Tom, well done for defeating Murk," Marc smiled, his robes swirling all about him. "It can't have been easy."

"I had some help," Tom replied, as Elenna, Silver and Storm joined him.

"Hello, Marc," Elenna said. Then she frowned. "How are Queen Romaine's preparations for battle? Are her forces powerful?"

Marc's face was serious. "Velmal's magic is strong. If she is going to succeed, you must get all the ingredients for the potion."

Tom handed over the enchanted weeds. "I liberated these from Murk."

"And you have brought us one step closer to defeating Velmal," Marc replied. "I must go now, but the best of luck with your next Quest." The young wizard began to fade before them.

"Where to now?" Elenna asked. "We only need two more ingredients."

But even as Elenna uttered these words, Tom felt a freezing fog curl around his body. The mist faded away to reveal the figures of his mother, Freya, and Velmal. The evil wizard's face was twisted into a sneer. In his hand he gripped his staff with its two glistening axe-blades.

The figures hovered just in front of Tom, and he felt rage surge through

him as he saw that Velmal had his
fingers in a cruel grip around the
back of Freya's neck. Her face was
pale and her eyes were half-closed, as
she swayed from side to side, barely
able to stand.

"Tom, save me," Freya whispered.
"I need you."

Emotion swamped Tom. This was the first time he'd ever heard his mother admit that she needed his help.

"How touching a mother's plea is!" Velmal laughed, his long hair whipping across his face. "Unfortunately, there is nothing you can do. Freya is completely under my control." He smiled. "And when she's dead I'll find another puppet, and there is nothing you can do about it!" Velmal laughed again and the figures disappeared as quickly as they materialized.

Tom turned to Elenna. "We have a Quest to complete," he managed to say.

Elenna nodded and they both climbed into Storm's saddle, ready to ride into the new dawn. As they galloped around the edge of the swamp, Tom could see their attacker with the eye-patch watching from behind a tree. He looked terrified.

"The Beast is gone," Tom called out to him. "Go back to your village and tell them that there is silver in this swamp." He took the fist-size nugget of silver from his pocket and tossed it in the man's direction.

The Kayonian's face broke out in a smile as he scrabbled for the silver. Then he mounted his horse and trotted away towards his village. No apology for attacking them or kidnapping Silver passed his lips.

"What a horrible man," Elenna said, watching him go.

"There are far worse things to face," Tom said. "We still have a Quest to finish and two Beasts to defeat. The stakes are higher than ever. Come on, let's go." Tom turned Storm towards the horizon and dug his heels into the stallion's side, urging his faithful friend onwards. Silver ran ahead, barking happily. For the first time in his life, his mother had said that she needed him... What else would the future hold? There was only one way of finding out.

"Forwards!" Tom cried.

Here's a sneak preview of Tom's
next exciting adventure!

Meet

Terra
CURSE OF THE
FOREST

Only Tom can free the Beasts from
Velmal's wicked enchantment...

PROLOGUE

With his axe balanced over his shoulder, Edric picked his way across the forest floor. The crunch of dry leaves beneath his feet sounded deafening; he even imagined he could hear his own heart thumping. Where were the birds in the trees and the animals rustling in the undergrowth?

Light poured down from the gaps between the branches, bathing patches of the forest in Kayonian sunshine. Ferns stirred in the light breeze and fungi ballooned around the tree trunks. This place would be beautiful, if it wasn't so deadly, Edric thought, shivering. Three of his friends had already ventured into the depths of the forest that month. None had returned.

You're mad, he told himself. You shouldn't have come.

But Edric had no choice. He wanted to find his friends, and his village needed more wood; the forest was the only place to get it. Without wood they could not fashion any more weapons, and without weapons, how could they ever hope to free themselves from the tyrannical Queen Romaine? Edric still didn't understand why the queen had turned on her people, but she certainly had to be stopped!

He took a swig from his flask and pressed on, watching the shadows warily. He told himself that the stories about the forest weren't true. Nothing lived here except for rabbits and deer.

Certainly no monsters!

Edric caught his foot in something and tripped, crying out as he fell to the mossy ground. It was just a gnarled root. Edric breathed a sigh of relief.

"Stop being silly," he said firmly. Steadying himself against a tree trunk, he rose to his feet.

Follow this Quest to the end in TERRA CURSE OF THE FOREST.

Win an exclusive
Beast Quest T-shirt and goody bag!

Tom has battled many fearsome Beasts and we want to know which one is your favourite! Send us a drawing or painting of your favourite Beast and tell us in 30 words why you think it's the best.

Each month we will select **three** winners to receive a Beast Quest T-shirt and goody bag!

Send your entry on a postcard to
BEAST QUEST COMPETITION
Orchard Books, 338 Euston Road, London NW1 3BH.

Australian readers should email:
childrens.books@hachette.com.au

New Zealand readers should write to:
Beast Quest Competition, 4 Whetu Place, Mairangi Bay,
Auckland NZ, or email: childrensbooks@hachette.co.nz

**Don't forget to include your name and address.
Only one entry per child.**

Good luck!

Join the Quest,
Join the Tribe

www.beastquest.co.uk

Have you checked out the Beast Quest website? It's the
place to go for games, downloads, activities, sneak
previews and lots of fun!

You can read all about your favourite beasts, download
free screensavers and desktop wallpapers for your
computer, and even challenge your friends
to a Beast Tournament.

Sign up to the newsletter at www.beastquest.co.uk
to receive exclusive extra content and the opportunity
to enter special members-only competitions. We'll send
you up-to-date info on all the Beast Quest books,
including the next exciting series which features
six brand-new Beasts!

FREE COLLECTOR CARDS INSIDE!

Series 6
BEAST QUEST

Can Tom and his companions rescue his mother
from the clutches of evil Velmal...?

KOMODO
978 1 40830 723 6

MURO
978 1 40830 724 3

FANG
978 1 40830 725 0

MURK
THE SWAMP MAN
978 1 40830 726 7

TERRA
CURSE OF THE FOREST
978 1 40830 727 4

VESPICK
THE WASP QUEEN
978 1 40830 728 1

CRETA
THE WINGED TERROR
978 1 40830 735 9

SPECIAL BUMPER EDITION!

Does Tom have the
strength to triumph
over cunning Creta?

Series 7: THE LOST WORLD
COMING SOON!

CONVOL
THE COLD-BLOODED BRUTE

978 1 40830 729 8

HELLION
THE FIERY FOE

978 1 40830 730 4

KRESTOR
THE CRUSHING TERROR

978 1 40830 731 1

MADARA
THE MIDNIGHT WARRIOR

978 1 40830 732 8

ELLIK
THE LIGHTNING HORROR

978 1 40830 733 5

CARNIVORA
THE WINGED SCAVENGER

978 1 40830 734 2

FROM THE DARK,
A HERO ARISES...

Dare to enter the kingdom of Avantia.

A dark land, where wild creatures roam
and people fight tooth-and-nail to
survive another day.

And now, as the prophecies warned, a new evil
arises. Lord Derthsin – power-hungry and driven
by hatred – has ordered his armies into the
four corners of Avantia. Just one flicker
of hope remains...

If the four Beasts of Avantia can find their
Chosen Riders – and unite them into a deadly
fighting force – they might have the strength
to challenge Derthsin. But if they fail, the
land of Avantia will be lost forever...

OUT JULY 2010

www.worldofavantia.com